Ghost Rescue

AND
MUTTERMAN'S ZOO

Ghost Rescue

AND
MUTTERMAN'S ZOO

WRITTEN BY
Andrew Murray

ILLUSTRATED BY
Sarah Horne

ORCHARD BOOKS

ORCHARD BOOKS
338 Euston Road, London NW1 3BH
Orchard Books Australia
Level 17/207 Kent Street, Sydney, NSW 2000
First published in hardback in Great Britain in 2009 by Orchard Books
First published in paperback in 2009
ISBN 978 1 84616 355 5 (hardback)
ISBN 978 1 84616 363 0 (paperback)
Text © Andrew Murray 2009
Illustrations © Sarah Horne 2009
The rights of Andrew Murray to be identified as the author and of
Sarah Horne to be identified as the illustrator of this work have been asserted by
them in accordance with the Copyright, Designs and Patents Act, 1988.
A CIP catalogue record for this book is available from the British Library.
1 3 5 7 9 10 8 6 4 2 (hardback)
1 3 5 7 9 10 8 6 4 2 (paperback)
Printed in Great Britain
Orchard Books is a division of Hachette Children's Books,
an Hachette UK company.
www.hachette.co.uk

It was boredom that led Charlie to watch daytime TV. There had been no emails asking for Ghost Rescue's help. Lord Fairfax was doing a ghost crossword with his ghost glasses perched on his nose and a ghost pencil in his hand.

The other members of Ghost Rescue –
Lord Fairfax's ghost wife Lady F, their
ghost daughter Florence, their ghost dog
Zanzibar and Rio the ghost parrot – were
trying not to disturb him. Which is when
Charlie, the only live member of Ghost
Rescue, turned on the TV and they all
saw the end of the news.

"And finally," said the newsreader, "monkey business at the City Zoo, where all the furry residents have started acting *very* strangely indeed. Our reporter, Arnie Smarmy, is there right now. What's going on, Arnie?"

"Well, Carl," the reporter replied, "I can hardly hear you for all the noise down here! The rhinos are moaning, the lions are groaning, the hyenas are howling and the sea lions are scowling. The keepers have tried everything to calm them down, but at the moment, Carl, this animal madness is a complete mystery..."

Lord F looked and, sitting up sharply, looked again.

"Goodness!" he said.

"What is it?" said Charlie.

"Ghosts!" said Lord F. "Animal ghosts by the dozen – I can see them in the background. There, over that patch of ground that looks like…what is it, an animal graveyard, maybe? It's *packed* with animal ghosts, and they're all jumping up and down, running this way and that. It looks like *they're* all howling and screeching, too."

Charlie leaned forward, and squinted, and then crawled right up to the TV screen. The ghosts were very faint, but he could just see them.

"Wow!" he said. "They're going absolutely crazy. They must be in some awful kind of pain or fear to be acting like that. And maybe the *living* animals can hear them, or sense them somehow, and that's what's making *them* go crazy too."

"Something's got to be done, Charlie,"
said Lord Fairfax, with a twinkle in his eye.

Charlie grinned at him. "Looks like a
job for Ghost Rescue..."

A few hours later the Ghostmobile, an old pizza delivery van that Charlie drove with the ghosts directing him, parked in the City Zoo car park. Charlie and the Fairfaxes went through the main gate and began to look around. And there, amid the bedlam of animal noise, was the strangest thing they had ever seen. It was an elephant.

We've all seen elephants before – but have you ever seen one trying to climb a tree? Shattered branches lay all around, evidence of his climbing attempts. In the end the elephant gave up and raised his trunk – but instead of trumpeting, he hooted and chattered. Then he sat on his backside, and with his forefeet tried, and failed, to peel a banana.

Utterly baffled, Ghost Rescue pressed on through the zoo — only to be suddenly faced by a lion! Charlie shrieked and looked for a place to hide — whereupon the lion squeaked, turned tail, and disappeared down a lion-sized burrow. They saw his frightened eyes glinting in the dark.

Then they moved on to the sea lion pool. There was a stirring in the water – and a camel surfaced, with a fish in its mouth…

How were they going to get to the bottom of all this very strange animal behaviour? Ghost Rescue decided to spy on the animal cemetery, which seemed empty to Charlie at first, but as he got closer he could just see the faint shapes of the animal ghosts, flapping and panicking.

Soon a man, dressed
in a Zoo uniform, crept
out to the graves
with a strange
contraption that
glowed and
hummed with
power. The
Fairfaxes vanished
and Charlie kept
out of sight as
they watched.

The man dug up a bone from a monkey's grave, and the monkey's ghost hooted in protest. The man slipped the bone into a tray at the base of the device, and pressed a big red button. *WHOOM!*

A shimmering force field burst out and enveloped the ghost, sucking it back inside the machine. The sides of the machine were transparent, and the members of Ghost Rescue could see the poor thing trapped inside the humming energy field. The man carried the contraption through a door marked "DANGER – NO ADMITTANCE".

Charlie and the Fairfax ghosts sneaked in through the door and found a laboratory straight out of a nightmare. The man, who wore a badge that read "Doctor Malvolio Mutterman, Head of  Research", was unloading the monkey ghost into a kind of holding cage, which glowed and hummed with the same eerie power as his machine. There the poor ghost monkey sat, hopping and hooting.

But it was not the only cage. Charlie's
eyes grew wide as he saw the rows of
cages stretching along the walls. Most
of them glowed and hummed and had
a miserable ghost cowering inside.

At the end of the lab was the strangest machine of all. There were two large booths, connected to a central control panel by all sorts of wires and pipes.

The whole thing throbbed with an awesome power, and gave off an overpowering smell of burnt electricity. One booth was empty, but in the other sat a terrified wild dog.

Doctor Mutterman was carrying a large aerosol can, marked "Spirit-Based Adhesive". He sprayed the stuff all over the poor creature, until it dripped with the strange, ghostly goo.

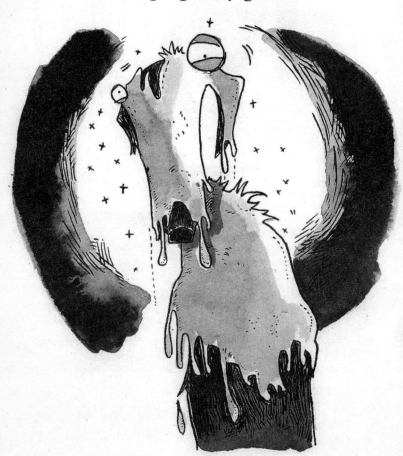

Doctor Mutterman went over to a cage holding the ghost of a parrot. Ghost Rescue saw that each cage was mounted on wheels.

Mutterman rolled the cage into the empty booth – it was a perfect fit – while the ghost parrot flapped and squawked. Rio and Zanzibar exchanged anxious looks.

Then Mutterman threw a switch, and the lab was filled with sparking and crackling. The throbbing rose to an insane shriek, and lights flashed all over the central control panel. Then there was a blinding flash, and Charlie and Ghost Rescue blinked and rubbed their eyes.

When they looked again, the parrot ghost had vanished from its booth. In the other booth, the dog had started to squawk and flap its forelegs, as if trying to fly.

Mutterman gave an insane cackle –
"*Hee-hya-hya-hya!*"

But Ghost Rescue, especially Rio the
ghost parrot and Zanzibar the ghost dog,
were horrified. What a monstrous scheme!

But as the team were pondering what to do next, Mutterman caught sight of Charlie and grabbed him.

"Well, well, a little spy! You want to see what's going on here, do you? Well, let me give you the best view in the house…"

Charlie kicked and bit, and his foot knocked over a jar of something on a workbench. But Mutterman had him now, and as the Fairfaxes watched in horror, he dragged Charlie over to the machine.

He opened the booth, releasing the
poor, flapping parrot-dog, and threw
Charlie into it instead.

"Why?" asked Charlie. "Why are you doing this?"

"Why? Oh poor, thick-witted boy, isn't it obvious? Don't you *see* what I am doing here – taking the spirit of one creature and letting it live again in the body of another? Now, thanks to me, when we grow old and sick, we can move to a new, young, healthy body – just as easily as moving house. I am answering the deepest dream of the human race – to *live forever!*"

"That's crazy," said Charlie. "If we all lived forever, the world would get so crowded. There'd be no room for anyone."

"Who said anything about *all* of us living forever?" sneered Mutterman. "My service will be available to all *who can pay*..." And he threw back his head and laughed – "*Hee-hya-hya-hya!*"

"Actually, boy," Mutterman continued, "you've come along at *just* the right time. My experiments on animals have been a *sensational* success. Now it is time to move on...to *humans*." Mutterman strolled along the rows of cages, with the wide variety of ghosts inside them.

"Ever wanted to be an eagle, boy? Or an otter, maybe? How about a mighty tiger? Hmm, let's see – ah! A monkey, of course, *hya-hya-hya*, perfect!"

Mutterman wheeled the monkey's
cage over to the machine, and slid it
into the
other booth.
He started
cranking up
the power
again, pressing
buttons and
flipping switches.

The Fairfaxes were in a panic.

"What can we *do?*" wailed Florence. "Hurry, think! There's no time to lose. Any moment now, Charlie will be peeling bananas and swinging from trees..."

Then Zanzibar started sniffing at the workbench.

"What's that dripping over the edge?" asked Florence.

"That's the stuff Charlie knocked over," said Lord Fairfax.

It looked familiar. They read the label on the jar: "Spirit-Based Adhesive".

"It's the stuff Mutterman sprayed all over the parrot ghost," said Lady Fairfax. "It must be the thing that sticks the ghost to its new body!"

"Well, that's all very interesting," said her husband, "but how is it going to help us rescue Charlie? We're just ghosts. If only we had *real* bodies, we could do something to save him…"

They stared at the adhesive, then stared at Mutterman. Suddenly they all had the same idea.

"*That's it!*"

And quickly they started rolling themselves in the spilled spirit glue, rubbing it in their hair and clothes, shuffling their feet in it and rubbing their hands in it, until they were dripping from head to toe in the stuff.

Then they all got ready. They looked at Mutterman as he fiddled with the machine. They took a deep breath.

"OK then — *last one in is a scaredy-ghost!*"

And they all charged at Mutterman, and dived towards him, at him, through him, *into* him… They disappeared inside his body, and they *stuck*. Mutterman yelped, and jumped, and shouted. But the voices were not Mutterman's any more.

His mouth opened, and Lord F's voice came out.

Good evening

He flapped his arms in just the way Rio flapped his wings.

His mouth opened again, and Lady F spoke.

His mouth opened a third time, and Zanzibar barked.

And his body jerked and twisted this way and that, as if six people were inside it with six different ideas of what it should be doing.

"Over to the booth! Get the hands working, come on now, all together – no, not *that* way, over *here*…!"

"I *am* going the right way, it's somebody else who's doing it wrong…"

"Who's working his feet? Oh, it's me, sorry, I can feel them now…"

"Ow, who's that? You're pinching. Careful, keep his balance now…"

"Woof, woof, woof!"

"Get — ow, argh! Curse you all! *Get — out — of — my — BODY!"*

"Awwwwwk!"

Mutterman was still there, of course, but he was outnumbered five to one in his own body. And despite his curses and protests, the Fairfaxes got the hang of moving him.

Clumsily, they made his hands open the booth and set Charlie free. Now it was time for Ghost Rescue to rescue some ghosts...

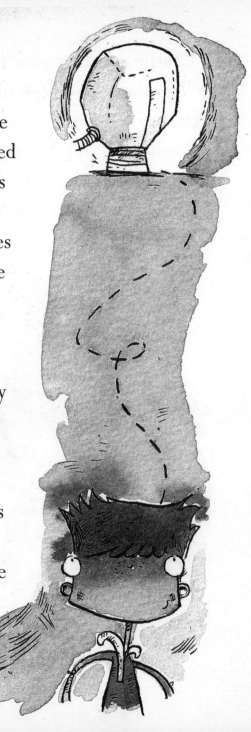

Charlie cut the power from the holding cages, and took the bone from each cage. He carried the bones back to the cemetery, and all the ghosts came along with him, hooting and barking and chirping – but with happiness this time.

Charlie carefully buried each bone in its rightful place – and the ghostly creatures could finally be at peace.

But this still left the problem of the dog possessed by the ghost parrot – and the camel haunted by the sea lion spirit, the lion haunted by the rabbit and the elephant possessed by the monkey. Not to mention the mad scientist with five ghosts stuck inside *him*.

"Mutterman, how do you unstick the spirit glue?" asked Charlie.

At first Mutterman wouldn't say. But the ghosts swung his arms and forced him to slap himself – *ow!* – again and again and again and—

"*Ow! Stop!* All right, all right, I'll tell you! Just stop hitting me, OK? There's another jar in the lab, full of spirit solvent, which will unstick the spirit glue – *OK?*"

So the Fairfaxes steered Mutterman's body, clumsily waving and stumbling, back to the lab. First, they had to grab the jar of spirit solvent...then lead the dog, elephant, lion and camel back to the cemetery, and pour the solvent over them... The parrot, monkey, rabbit and sea lion ghosts came unstuck, and gratefully returned to their graves.

The dog, lion and camel wanted nothing
more to do with this madness,
and scurried away to
their enclosures.

But the elephant marched over to the laboratory door. An elephant never forgets, and this one seemed to have unfinished business. They all followed as the elephant barged into the lab, and saw the hated cages and machine.

He went *crazy*, trampling and trumpeting, stamping with his great feet and swinging his tusks and trunk. The lab was smashed to pieces. Then, satisfied at last, the elephant strolled happily back to the elephant house and munched on his supper of cabbages, carrots and hay — but *definitely* not bananas…

Finally, Charlie poured the spirit solvent over Mutterman, and the Fairfaxes were so relieved to come unstuck from him.

"*Ohh*, free at last!"

"Thank goodness! Mutterman's body is a nice place to visit, but I wouldn't want to live there."

"*Woof!*"

"*Awwk!*"

Mutterman just collapsed in a wretched heap as he contemplated his wrecked laboratory, his shattered dreams.

But Charlie warned him, "Beware, Mutterman — Ghost Rescue will be watching the news, and if any more funny business happens, *we'll come to get you!*"

As Mutterman sat among the wreckage, the Ghostmobile drove away from the Zoo, and a hundred ghostly animal voices hooted, and squawked, and barked their goodbyes.

WRITTEN BY
Andrew Murray

ILLUSTRATED BY
Sarah Horne

All priced at £3.99

The Ghost Rescue books are available from all good bookshops,
or can be ordered direct from the publisher:
Orchard Books, PO BOX 29, Douglas IM99 1BQ
Credit card orders please telephone 01624 836000
or fax 01624 837033 or visit our website: www.orchardbooks.co.uk
or email: bookshop@enterprise.net for details.

To order please quote title, author and ISBN
and your full name and address.
Cheques and postal orders should be made payable to 'Bookpost plc'.
Postage and packing is FREE within the UK
(overseas customers should add £1.00 per book).

Prices and availability are subject to change.